Miles' Piano Lesson

Miles to go Before I sleep

Vol. 1

story and illustrations by

Monica Charles

This book is dedicated to

Miles, Amare, Misahra and Myla.

Doe, Re, Me, Fa, Sol, La, Ti, Doe!!! Bang! Bang! Bang!

Miles's mom hurries from the kitchen to see who was making the noise on the piano. She looks into the living room and walks over to her son with a grin on her face.

"Baby, what are you doing?"

"I'm playing the piano, Mom," Miles responds with a funny smirk on his face.

"Oh really? Well, I know someone who can give you piano lessons and make you sound even better. With practice you can be as good as Ray Charles or Thomas Bethune."

"Who?" Miles begins to imagine playing the piano and everyone coming to hear him play.

Then, he thought about how much harder it would be if he couldn't see. How could he find the keys? He figures Ray and Thomas must have had magic fingers to do something so great.

Miles' mom interrupts his daydreaming "Miles, later we can read about them and listen to some of my Ray Charles CD's. Can you get dressed and play outside while I get this house clean and then I'll make you some lunch?"

"Sure, Mom!" Miles answers.

He jumps off the bench and races upstairs to get ready. Miles puts on his blue jeans and his favorite Red T-shirt that has the letter "M" on it. He is almost out of his room when he realizes someone very important is missing. He goes to the shelf in his room, reaches up high, and grabs an orange and green triceratops named Phil.

Now, Miles is ready to go and play in the backyard.

Swoosh!!! Swoosh!!

Miles is flying Phil in the air like he is a dinosaur airplane when, suddenly, he sees a fiery red bird coming straight towards him.

Miles ducks down as the bird yells, "Watch out!"

It lands in the big maple tree. Miles runs quickly to see if the bird is okay. The bird flies out of the tree and lands on a branch near Miles.

"Sorry I scared you. It is very windy today and I was rushing to get here. My name is Robin. " Nice to meet you, Miles."

Miles looks in amazement and says, "Nice to meet you, Robin. Why were you rushing to see me?"

"I was sent here from the heavens to give you a special gift." Robin lifts up his wing and a black, red, and green key land in Miles' hands.

"This is the key of knowledge and it unlocks a special door to the past.   Once you enter, you will go on a journey and find the answers to anything your mind can think of." Robin flies above Phil and colorful sprinkles from her wings cover him.

"Phil will come to life in the land of the past to help and protect you."

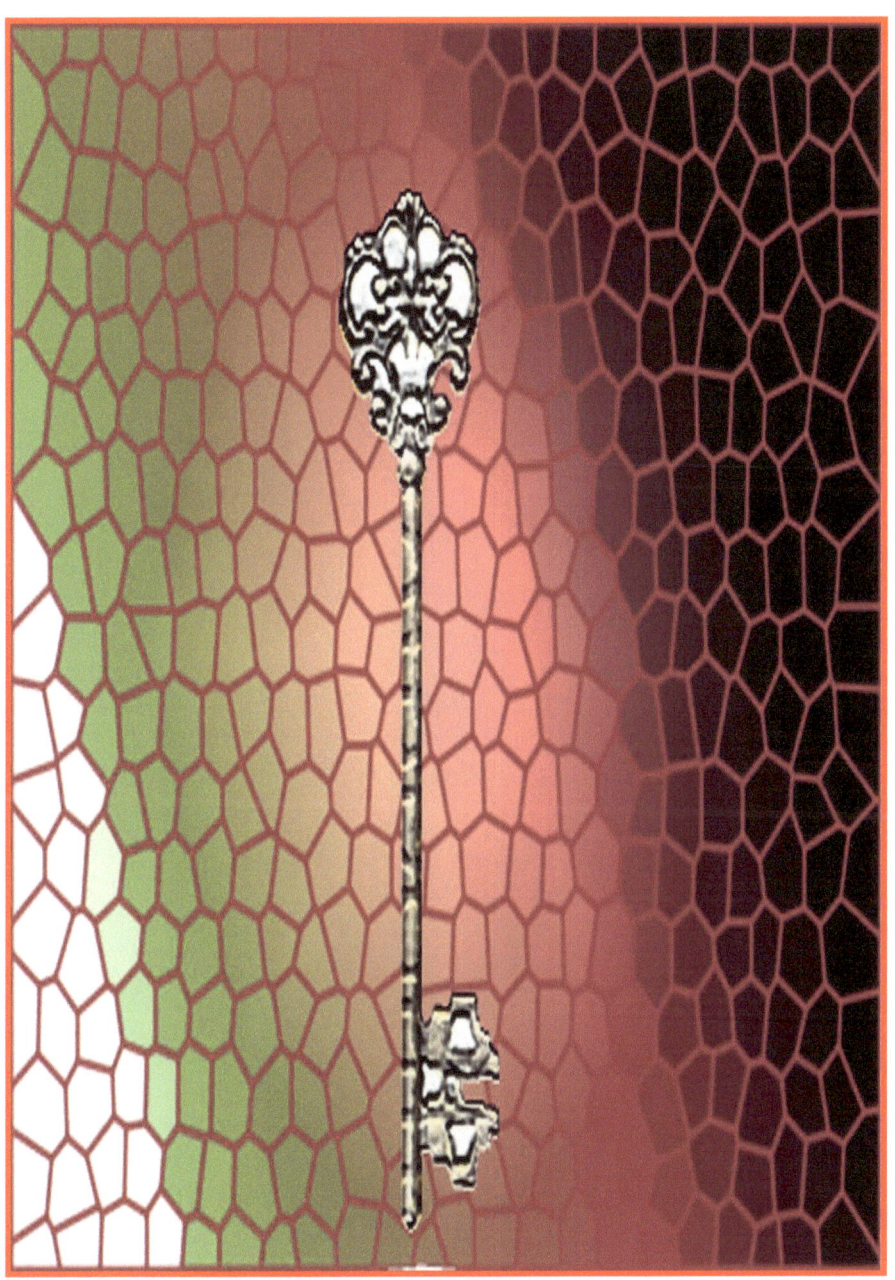

Miles can't wait to get started and knows exactly what he wants to find out first. "I want to know more about playing the piano. This is going to be so cool! I can't wait to start! Where is the Door?"

Miles feels a warm breeze and then someone whispering, "Pssst, over here." He turns around and sees a door. It is a big wooden door with friendly eyes and a doorknob with a keyhole. "Hey, Miles, I'm Doreen. Whenever you look and ask for me I will appear."

"Wow!" Miles says with excitement.

Miles is about to put the key in the hole and Robin yells, "Wait! I almost forgot. Watch out for Clarabelle the Chameleon. She is evil and wants to take the key of knowledge so you can't learn. She can transform herself into objects and camouflage with any background. Don't worry though; Phil will be there to protect you and as long as you truly want to learn you will always defeat her."

"Thanks, Robin! I'm ready now," Miles sighs with relief.

Miles and Phil go through the door, on their journey to learn about the piano.

Miles opens the door and sees a beautiful garden with a golden path right in the middle. As Miles begins to walk with Phil by his side, they come across a rainbow colored piano.

Miles starts to bang on the keys and, suddenly, the piano laughs and turns into a chameleon with indigo eyes and a red snake-like tongue.

"Oh no!" Miles yells as the chameleon walks around him in a circle, coming closer and closer.

It is Clarabelle the Chameleon. Robin had warned him about her. As Clarabelle comes closer to Miles, she says, "Why do you want to learn about the piano? Why do you want to learn anything? You should focus on playing and things that don't require your mind to work so hard. You know a mind is a terrible thing to use."

"Hmmm, I thought the saying was: a mind is a terrible thing to waste?" Miles responds.

Clarabelle hisses with anger, leaps and tries to take Miles's key from around his neck. Miles falls to the floor. Phil leaps in front of Miles and begins to roar so loud that Clarabelle is frightened and turns white with fear. She crawls quickly into the garden until she is out of sight.

Miles and Phil continue their journey, hoping never to see Clarabelle again, but they both have a feeling it would not be the last time.

They follow the golden path and come across a man with a cane. He is wearing shades and a black suit. He is sitting on a Cliff note shaped fountain that is flowing with milk and honey.

"Hey, Miles and Phil. My name is Thomas Bethune, but you can call me Tom. Follow me."

"Where are we going?" asks Miles, following Tom.

"We are going to meet my friend Ray so that we can teach you how to play the piano. Ray and I have a lot in common. We are both blind, love shades, can play the piano very well, and are among the greatest piano players in the world. We lived during different times but are well remembered for the things we did."

Thomas Greene Bethune (Blind Tom)
(1849 - 1908)

"Like what?" Miles questions. He is very curious.

"I was playing the piano and writing music during the 1800's. I could play the piano by the age of six. I was born a slave, which means I was not free to go and do whatever I wanted. What gave me some freedom was my talent for playing the piano. Because I was so good, I was allowed to tour around the world, playing for people everywhere. I wrote over a hundred songs and played for President Buchanan at the White House."

"You went to the White House and met a president. I wish I could do that." Miles says.

RAY CHARLES

(1930 -2004)

"Young man, you can do whatever you want to do. Just believe.

"Now, Ray was born in the 1900s. He has won Grammy's, Lifetime Achievement Awards, acted in movies, and so much more. Ray not only played the piano, he composed, recorded and sang his own songs. He first started playing when he was around your age too."

"Wow, I can't wait to meet him!" Miles says.

"Well, here we are," Tom replies.

Miles looks at this huge house, shaped like a piano. The windows are in the shape of musical notes and

the air is filled with tunes. Miles wonders how much fun it would be to live in a house like this one.

Tom opens the door and Ray is in the living room playing and singing a song Miles has never heard before.   All of a sudden Miles can't control himself. The music sounds so good Miles has to clap his hands, move his feet, and shake all over.

Ray feels Miles's presence and starts chuckling. "Hi, Miles, come sit on the bench here and let me show you how to play some notes on this piano."

Miles can't believe it. He is finally going to have his first lesson with one of the best piano players in the world! How cool is this? he thinks.

Miles hops on the seat and Ray begins showing him the basic keys on the piano and how the pedals work. Ray is careful not to confuse Miles by showing him too much.

"Miles, if it's okay with you, I would like to play a song in honor of your visit today," Ray says.

"Sure," Miles says.

Ray begins to play and Miles is mesmerized by what he hears.

And when this life is over, remember I was singing this song to you

Ray finishes and Miles gives him a big hug.

"Thanks, Ray, this is great. I can't wait to get back and tell all my friends about today," Miles says. He looks out the window and sees it is getting late. "Oh, I think it's time for Phil and me to get back home."

"Okay, well, next time I will show you how to play with your back facing the piano. So, make sure you keep practicing," Tom says. He grabs his coat and leads Miles and Phil back down the path toward home.

Miles and Phil hug Tom and thank him for everything.

"Remember, we are always here because we are a part of your past, and when you need us we are there inside of you, right in your heart," Tom says.

Miles nods and is a little sad to be leaving them. He is happy to know that he can always visit his new friends when he really misses them.

Miles and Phil step back through the door and are back in the future, in the middle of their yard again. Miles is puzzled because it is still daylight. He checks his watch and the time had not changed. He looks at his stuffed animal and starts to wonder if he has been daydreaming.

He hears mom calling, "Miiiiiiles! Lunch is readyyyy!"

"Coming, Mama!" Miles responds.

As Miles starts towards the house, he sees the Robin flying in the sky. He reaches in his pocket and finds the red, green and black key. Miles looks behind him and realizes it definitely was not a dream. He can't wait for his next adventure in learning about anything and everything. He enters the house, his head filled with thoughts of piano keys and dreams!